Claudia
the Accessories Fairy

by Daisy Meadows

Jack Frost's Ice Castle

Up to the Roof Garden Cafe

LIFT

Ice cream parlour

Marshing Town

COMFY FEET

WINTER WOOLIES

Beautiful YOU!

SNIP & CLIP

Central Fountain

Press booth

Bath Bliss

...aurant.

Jack Frost's Spell

I'm the king of designer fashion,
Looking stylish is my passion.
Ice Blue's the name of my fashion range,
Some people think my clothes are strange.

Do I care, though? Not a bit!
My designer label will be a hit.
The Fashion Fairies' magic will make that come true:
Soon everyone will wear Ice Blue!

Contents

A Hole Lot
of Trouble

"Here we are," Mr Walker said, parking the car at *Tippington Fountains Shopping Centre*. He glanced over to where his daughter Rachel and her best friend Kirsty Tate were sitting in the back seat. "I know you only came here yesterday, girls, but I need to pick up a shirt. I'll be as quick as I can."

"Don't worry, Dad," Rachel said, exchanging a secret smile with Kirsty as they got out of the car. "We don't mind at all. Take as long as you like!"

It was the second day of half-term, and Kirsty was staying with Rachel's family. Whenever the two friends got together, magical things always seemed to happen – and they certainly had yesterday! Rachel's mum had brought the girls here to the shopping centre, as it was the grand opening day, with lots of free activities to take part in, and a whole procession of colourful floats. It had all been really fun and exciting… especially when the girls had found themselves whisked off to Fairyland, and thrown into an exciting, brand-new fairy adventure. Hurrah!

"I hope we meet another fairy today," Kirsty whispered eagerly to Rachel, as they made their way through the car park to the lifts.

"Oh, me too," Rachel replied.
"Yesterday was amazing. But you know
what Queen Titania always says: we
can't go looking for magic. We have to
wait for it to come to us." She grinned.
"I just hope it finds us again soon, that's
all!"

The three of them went up in the lift.

"Ground floor," a voice
from the speaker
announced after
a few moments.
"Welcome to
*Tippington
Fountains Shopping
Centre!*"
The doors opened
to reveal the shopping
mall before them.

The shop fronts sparkled with smart chrome fittings, glass elevators rose smoothly between floors and a large central fountain played in the middle of a wide blue pool, surrounded by smaller fountains. Rachel smiled as she and Kirsty gazed at the fountain display.

That was the spot where they'd seen Phoebe the Fashion Fairy yesterday, and their new fairy adventure had begun.

They'd met Phoebe before of course
– they'd had a very exciting adventure
with her when they'd helped all the
Party Fairies on a secret mission. But
Kirsty and Rachel hadn't realised that
Phoebe had a whole team of Fashion
Fairies, who assisted her throughout the
fairy kingdom and the human world.

Yesterday, Phoebe had invited the girls
to Fairyland to see the special fairy
fashion show they were putting on. And
that was when everything had gone
wrong…

Kirsty shuddered as she remembered
how Jack Frost and his naughty goblins
had turned up uninvited to the show, and
proceeded to throw the whole thing into
chaos. Dressed in outfits from his own
clothing label, Ice Blue, Jack Frost had

used a bolt of icy magic to steal seven
magical objects belonging to the Fashion
Fairies. Kirsty and Rachel had gone on
to help Miranda the Beauty Fairy rescue
her magic lipstick, which ensured that
everyone had a beautiful smile. But there
were still six magic objects left to find.

"What do you think
of this hat, girls?" Mr
Walker said, jolting
Kirsty out of her
thoughts. She and
Rachel turned
to see that he'd
stopped at *Winter
Woollies* and was
holding up a black
beanie hat.

"It looks just what I need to keep my

head warm now that the weather's turned colder."

"I like it," Rachel said. "Why don't you try it on?"

Mr Walker pulled the hat onto his head…but to their surprise, his head went right through the top of it.

"Oh!" he cried, startled. "This hasn't been made very well." He took the hat off to reveal a great big hole in the woolly knitting. "How strange," he said. "I didn't notice that before."

The lady on the stall looked taken aback too. "I'm so sorry," she said. "There must have been a fault in that one. Do try another."

But when Mr Walker tried a second hat on – a navy-blue one, this time – the same thing happened again. And he wasn't the only person to have a problem. A woman nearby had just bought a thick red scarf. But by the time she'd wrapped it around her neck, the wool had unravelled to leave long dangling strings at each end!

"I don't understand," the lady on the stall said, turning pink and looking flustered. "I'm so sorry. There must be a faulty batch. Let me find you another scarf."

Rachel and Kirsty exchanged a look. Could this have something to do with the Fashion Fairies' missing magical objects?

Then Kirsty glanced down at her

watch and gasped. "Look, Rachel," she whispered, pointing. "The hands on my watch are moving backwards. Something *very* weird is going on!"

Magic Sparkles

The girls stared at Kirsty's watch as the second hand ticked the wrong way around the face. That *was* odd. "It definitely feels as if there's some magic in the air," Rachel whispered. "Magic that isn't working very well. We've got to investigate!"

Rachel went over to her dad, who was now trying on a third hat. "Dad, can Kirsty and I go off on our own for a bit?" she asked.

"Of course," Mr Walker said, just as the hat split along the seam. "I'm not having much luck with hats today, that's for sure," he grumbled, taking it off again. He glanced up at a large clock on the wall of the shopping centre. "Shall I meet you back here in an hour?"

The girls agreed and waved goodbye, keeping an eye out for other strange happenings as they walked along.

"We could start looking for things to use in our outfits for the Design-and-Make Competition while we're here," Kirsty suggested.

"Good idea," Rachel said. "Then we can make them this afternoon, ready for tomorrow."

At the grand opening of the centre the day before, a famous model, Jessica Jarvis, had announced a special competition for children to design and make their own outfits. Tomorrow afternoon, those taking part had to show the clothes they'd created to the judges, and the winning designers would get to wear the outfits in a charity fashion show at the end of the week.

"I think I'll make something rainbow-coloured and sparkly," Rachel said thoughtfully. "It'll remind me of our very first magical adventure with the Rainbow Fairies – and all the wonderful fairy friends we've made ever since."

"That sounds great," Kirsty said. "I might make a dress out of floaty scarves sewn together. Something bright and patterned would be nice."

"Let's look in here," Rachel suggested, pointing to a nearby shop called *Finishing Touch*.

The friends walked towards the shop, just as two teenage girls came out. One had a pretty new bag on her shoulder and the other was fastening a new necklace around her neck. But just then, the strap on the first girl's bag broke, sending the bag tumbling to the ground. And seconds later, the other girl's necklace snapped, and shiny purple beads cascaded down, scattering everywhere!

"Oh no!" the girls cried. "How did *that* happen?"

Kirsty and Rachel
ran to help pick
up the fallen
beads, but
it was no
use. The
necklace was
beyond repair.

"Come on, let's get a refund," one of
the teenagers said as they went back
into the shop. "Brand-new accessories
shouldn't just fall apart like that!"

Rachel and Kirsty followed them inside,
and Kirsty headed for a rack of scarves.
To her disappointment, the only colour
scarf in stock seemed to be blue – there
was nothing remotely like the brightly
coloured patterns she'd hoped to find.

Rachel, too, was finding the shop rather

a let down. The jewellery seemed to
have lost its sparkle and some pieces had
missing stones or broken clasps. None of
it was right for the outfit she had in mind
for the competition.

"This is really weird," she heard the
shop assistant saying in confusion. "All
our accessories looked beautiful when I
set them out this morning. But somehow
they've become dull or broken since
then."

Rachel headed towards a display of necklaces. Surely there would be *some* sparkly jewellery? She quickened her pace as she spotted something glinting from between the beads but then, as she put a hand towards the necklaces, she almost jumped out of her skin. The sparkly jewel she thought she'd seen *wasn't* a jewel at all. In fact, it had just flown right off the necklace and into the air.

Rachel gasped in delight as she realised what she was looking at. A fairy!

The Search Begins

"Hello!" said the fairy, smiling at Rachel. She was wearing a sparkly purple puffball skirt, a pink top and a delicate blue cardigan, topped off with elegant bangles and an alice band with a big flower. Rachel recognised her as Claudia the Accessories Fairy, one of the seven Fashion Fairies she and Kirsty had met the day before.

31

"Hello," Rachel replied, smiling back. She glanced around to find Kirsty, who was still looking through the rack of blue scarves.

"Kirsty!" she whispered. "Over here!"

Kirsty's eyes lit up when she saw Claudia hovering in midair, a bright spark of light in the gloomy shop. She hurried over immediately.

"Hi," she whispered. "Claudia, isn't it? Nice to see you again!"

"Nice to see you too," Claudia said, her wings twinkling as they fluttered.

"I really need your help, girls. Since Jack Frost took my necklace, its powerful magic has gone into reverse. Instead of making sure that fashion accessories look perfectly pretty, the magic is working the other way, so that they look horrible. Even worse, they keep breaking and falling apart!"

"So that's why all those hats were torn," Rachel worked out. "And why the teenagers' bag and necklace broke earlier too."

"And that must be why my watch seems to be telling time backwards," Kirsty realised. "What a mess! We'll definitely help you look for your necklace, Claudia."

"Thank you," beamed the little fairy, flitting up to balance on a rack of necklaces. "Well, I've looked all over this shop and it certainly isn't here. And unfortunately, until it's back where it belongs, with me, everyone's accessories will become ruined. We've got to keep looking!"

34

Just then, the three of them heard a
loud voice coming from outside the shop.

"Come to the Ice Blue stall for the last
word in fashion!" it boasted.

Kirsty, Rachel and Claudia stiffened
at the words. Ice Blue? That was the
label Jack Frost had given to his line
of clothing. Surely it couldn't be a
coincidence?

They rushed to the entrance and went
outside to see what was going on.

There was Jack Frost himself, shouting
into a megaphone and dressed head to
toe in a silvery-blue outfit. His jacket
had spikes on the shoulders and elbows,
and there was a frosty pattern on his
trousers. He was standing in front of a
stall decorated with blue banners and
piled high with lots of different blue
accessories.

"Wow – he's a fast worker," Kirsty marvelled. "That stall wasn't even there when we came into the shop two minutes ago."

"He must have used magic to help set it up," Claudia whispered from where she was hiding in Rachel's pocket. "So maybe he's got my magic necklace – let's go and see!"

The girls left the shop with Claudia peeping out of Rachel's pocket. There was already a crowd around Jack Frost's stall, rummaging through the hats, scarves, badges, keyrings, bags, purses and jewellery on sale there. All of the products had the same logo, which was a bright blue silhouette of Jack Frost, showing off his big pointy nose and spiky beard.

"No need to push, there's plenty

for everyone!" called one of the stall assistants, and Kirsty nudged Rachel as she noticed that the assistants had green skin and long noses. They were goblins! All of them wore matching T-shirts with the same Jack Frost logo, and were very busy, dealing with so many customers at once.

Taking care not to be noticed by Jack Frost or the goblins, the girls squeezed through the crowds and pretended they

were customers too. They searched
through the boxes of necklaces hoping
to spot a magical shimmer, which would
mean Claudia's necklace was among
them.

"Those are very nice blue jeans," one
of the goblins said,
casting a sly look
at Rachel from
under his Ice
Blue baseball
cap. "Ice Blue is
the place to come
if you're looking for

the very best blue accessories, you know."

"Shame about your nasty red skirt
and top though, miss," a second goblin
said rudely to Kirsty. "We haven't got
anything to match *those*. Yuck!"

Kirsty felt annoyed at the goblin's rudeness but knew she mustn't draw attention to herself by arguing. Biting her tongue, she turned away and looked at a different part of the stall.

"Girls, let's go," Claudia whispered from Rachel's pocket. "I don't think the necklace is here, after all."

Rachel and Kirsty struggled to get out of the crowd, which was now even bigger than before. Once they were a safe distance away, Rachel asked, "Why don't you think the necklace was on the stall, Claudia? It was definitely Jack Frost and his goblins working there."

"I know, but didn't you hear what the goblin said?" Claudia asked. "They didn't have anything to match Kirsty's top. Yet my necklace should make sure that there are *always* matching accessories, even if the rest of its magic isn't working properly." She gave a little sigh of frustration. "That means the necklace must be somewhere else... But where?"

Follow That Goblin!

As the girls stood discussing where to try next, Rachel noticed a new goblin arriving at the stall, carrying boxes of Ice Blue merchandise.

"Coming through, coming through," he shouted, shoving irritably through the customers. "More amazing accessories coming through!"

One of the goblins on the stall looked relieved to see the newcomer. "About time," he snapped. "What took you so long? We've already sold out of baseball caps. Here, take this empty box away with you."

"I wonder where they're getting all those accessories from?" Rachel asked the other two. "They must be using magic to make them so quickly, don't you think, Claudia?"

Claudia brightened. "You're right," she said. "Magic from my necklace, I bet!"

"Let's follow the goblin and see where he goes," Kirsty suggested. "If we can find out where the Ice Blue accessories are coming from, we might find the necklace too."

"Good thinking," Claudia agreed. "But we mustn't let the goblins see us or they'll get suspicious. I'll turn you both into fairies, then it'll be easier for us all to stay out of sight. Let's find a quiet spot so I can work some magic."

The girls didn't need telling twice. They both loved being fairies — there was nothing to beat fluttering your wings and taking off into the air!

45

Kirsty and Rachel quickly huddled behind a large Ice Blue display, then Claudia waved her wand, sending a stream of purple sparkles tumbling into the air. The magic sparkles swirled all around the girls and in the next moment, they felt themselves shrinking smaller and smaller, until they were the same size as Claudia. They were fairies again! Joyfully fluttering their shimmering wings, they soared into the air after the goblin with the empty cardboard box.

The goblin turned into a deserted
alleyway and the three friends quietly
followed him through the back door of a
building. They hid in a high, dark corner
as he pressed a button on the wall to call
the lift, then slipped into the lift behind
him, taking care not to be seen.

The goblin pressed a button marked
"B", and the lift plunged downwards.

"Basement floor," came a robotic voice once it had stopped moving. Then the doors juddered apart, and the goblin walked out.

Kirsty, Rachel and Claudia flew after him and found themselves in a large workshop, full of goblins busily working noisy machines. They flitted up to a cobwebbed corner and perched on a ceiling beam to get a better view of the room.

"Goodness – they've set up a *factory* to make the Ice Blue accessories," Kirsty said under her breath. She stared at the rows of goblins using sewing machines, plastic moulds, scissors and glue guns. Elsewhere, there were massive rolls of blue fabric and boxes of the finished products stacked in piles.

"Jack Frost must have used his ice magic to make all this equipment," Claudia said, looking dazed. "He really *is* serious about his fashion company, isn't he? He obviously wants everyone to look just like him."

Rachel let out a little cry of excitement as she noticed something. "Look!" she whispered. "The goblin in charge – he's wearing your magic necklace, Claudia!"

True Blue, Through and Through!

There was no disguising the magic necklace. It shimmered with all the colours of the rainbow as it hung around the neck of the tallest goblin, who was bossing everyone else around. "Keep moving on those hats, guys," he yelled down one aisle of the workshop. "How are we doing on gloves? Let me check the quality."

Kirsty, Rachel and Claudia watched
him stride down to the glove-making
table where he angrily snatched up a
pair of gloves. "*Green* gloves? Weren't you
listening to Jack Frost? Everything's got
to be blue, you numbskulls. You'll have to
throw these away and start again."

The goblins at the
glove-making table
looked disgruntled.
"But we like
green," one of
them said sulkily.
"It's much better
than blue."

"No arguing!"
snapped the tall goblin.
"While I'm wearing this magic necklace,
I'm in charge, so you'll do as I say.

Now get on with some blue gloves at once – or I'll tell Jack Frost how lazy you are!"

Listening to their conversation gave Kirsty an idea. "Claudia, could you use your fairy magic to disguise me and Rachel as goblin workers?" she asked. "I'm wondering if, between us, we can possibly make the supervisor decide he doesn't want to be in charge any more."

Rachel's eyes lit up. "Oh yes!" she giggled. "And once he takes that necklace off…"

"I'll pounce!" Claudia finished with a grin. "Let's give it a try. If we go back to the lift area, I can turn you both into goblins!"

They flew quietly out of the workshop and back into the lift where nobody could see them. Then Claudia waved her wand and there was a bright flash of magic and a cloud of purple smoke.

When the smoke cleared, Kirsty and Rachel laughed as they saw that they now looked just like the other goblins on the factory floor. "Time to get to work," Kirsty grinned.

"Or rather, time to stir up some trouble!" Rachel replied, with a wink.

The two of them split up and joined the other goblins, who were working busily. Kirsty went to the assembly line, where a team of goblins were producing scarves, while Rachel went to the jewellery-making table nearby.

"I'm not keen on all this blue, you know," Kirsty muttered to the goblins closest to her. "I'd much rather wear a *green* scarf, wouldn't you?

Goblin green – everyone knows *that's* the best colour, right?"

"Goblin green is definitely *my* favourite colour," agreed a grumpy-looking goblin with pointy ears.

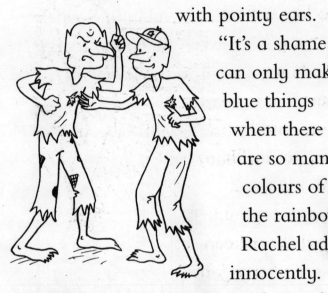

"It's a shame we can only make blue things when there are so many colours of the rainbow," Rachel added innocently.

"You'd look really handsome in purple, for example," she said, pointing to the goblin nearest to her. "And as for you – well, a yellow scarf or hat would really bring out the colour of your eyes."

She said this to a small, shy-looking
goblin and he blushed with pride.

"Do you think so?"
he said happily.
"I do like yellow,
I must say."

"Red's my
favourite
colour," another
goblin put in. "It
makes me think
of strawberry jam.
And whoever heard of
blue strawberry jam?"

Soon all the goblins were joining in:
"Green's definitely best."

"I'd like brown, to match my teeth."

"Orange clothes look brilliant on green
skin, I always think."

57

The supervisor was starting to look fed up. He blew a whistle to make everyone stop talking. "That's enough!" he roared. "You're meant to be working, not chatting. Silence!"

Kirsty dropped her scissors with a clatter. "I'm not doing any more work unless we can use different colours," she said daringly.

"Nor me," Rachel agreed, folding her arms. "I'm going on strike."

As she said the words, she felt her heart thump. If all the other goblins went meekly back to work, then their plan would fail. She and Kirsty might even be thrown out of the workshop – and then they'd have no chance of getting the necklace.

Thankfully, it seemed the goblins had had enough of being bossed around too. All across the workshop, there came the clatter of tools being put down and every single goblin put their nose in the air.

"I'm not working either," said one.

"We want colours!" said another.

"We want colours, we want colours!" chorused another group of goblins, stamping their feet in rhythm.

In a matter of seconds, the entire goblin workforce were chanting along and stamping their feet. "We want colours, we

want colours!"

One of the goblins pulled open a large cupboard and took out rolls of bright fabric. "Spots! Stripes! Flowers!" he cried happily.

"Red! Yellow! Green! Purple!" other goblins yelled, snatching up the fabrics

they wanted to use.

The supervisor looked close to tears.
Kirsty felt a bit sorry for him, but she
knew they had to stick to their plan
if they were to
get Claudia's
necklace
back.

"Oh
dear, Jack
Frost's not
going to
be happy if
he comes in
and sees what's
happening here," she
said loudly.

"And to think he trusted you with
the magic necklace," Rachel said to the

supervisor, shaking her head. "He's going to be *especially* cross with you!"

"I can't bear it any more!" the supervisor yelled, wrenching the necklace from around his neck. "I quit!"

Finishing Touches

Several goblins made a grab for the magic necklace as the supervisor took it off, but Claudia was too quick for them all. She darted in, grabbed the necklace and flew out of reach, much to the goblins' surprise. "The game's up, boys," she said sweetly as the necklace shrank down to fairy-size. Then she waved her wand, and the Ice Blue accessories turned to all the colours of the rainbow.

The goblins cheered…but then their faces fell as they realised what this meant for them.

"Jack Frost is going to be so mad with us," one gulped. "Quick – let's get back to Fairyland before he sees what we've done." And in the next moment, all the goblins had hurried out of the room… apart from two goblins who were rapidly changing back into girls.

Kirsty and
Rachel beamed
as Claudia
flew three
loops with
happiness.
"Thank
you so
much, girls!"
she said, as
she floated
down towards
them. "Your plan
was genius. Now
let's head back to the accessories shop
where we met, and I'll make sure that
everything in there looks gorgeous again,
with the help of my magic necklace."

As soon as Rachel and Kirsty were

back in the shopping centre, they realised that Claudia's magic was already working. The crowds had vanished from around the Ice Blue stall and they saw Jack Frost desperately bellowing into his megaphone, trying to attract customers. When it was clear that nobody was coming to buy anything, he flung the megaphone to the ground and stomped off furiously. "I'll make everyone wear Ice Blue somehow or other," he fumed.

"Not today, you won't," Claudia said with a smile, once he was out of earshot. She tucked herself in Kirsty's pocket as they went into the *Finishing Touch* store again, and Kirsty noticed with excitement that swirls of sparkly fairy magic were coming from Claudia's necklace and spreading around all the accessories.

In the blink of an eye, the shop was transformed. Gone were the dull, broken accessories, and in their place were colourful scarves, hats, bags and jewellery.

"That's *much* better," Claudia smiled. "I'd better fly now, girls. Thanks again. And good luck with the fashion competition tomorrow. You know we Fashion Fairies will be rooting for you!"

"Bye, Claudia,"
Rachel said. "Hope
we see you again
soon."

"Goodbye,"
Kirsty added.
"And thank you. I
know making my
costume is going to
be much easier now
there are so many pretty
scarves to choose from!"

Claudia vanished in a swirl of glittering
fairy dust and Kirsty remembered to
check her watch. "It's working again!"
she said in relief. "Oh, but we've only got
fifteen minutes before we meet your dad,
Rachel. We'd better choose something for
our outfits and head off."

"I know just what I'm going to do for mine," Rachel said, picking up a pack of glittery fabric paints. "After today, I'm tired of wearing blue. I'm going to make these jeans extra special by adding a few rainbow-coloured patterns on them."

"Brilliant idea," Kirsty said, sorting through the rack of scarves. She held up some striped scarves in bright colours.

"And these are perfect for my dress. Hurrah!"

Once they'd paid for the scarves and paints, the two happy friends set off to meet Mr Walker. They had the Design-and-Make Competition tomorrow *and* the fashion show at the end of the week to look forward to.

"Oh, and look," Rachel said, pointing to a sign that had just been put up in the shopping centre. "There's a Design-and-Make Competition workshop on here tomorrow morning. That sounds fun too. What a busy week we're having!"

"Fun, fairies and fashion – it sounds perfect to me," Kirsty laughed. "I can't wait to see what happens next!"

**Now it's time for Kirsty and
Rachel to help...**

Tyra the Dress Designer Fairy

Read on for a sneak peek...

"I can't wait for the Design-and-Make
Competition workshop to start," said
Kirsty Tate, peering into her bag in
excitement. "I've got my colourful scarves
and I'm going to sew them into a floaty
dress."

"It will be great!" said her best friend
Rachel Walker. "I'm going to paint a
glittery rainbow on my old jeans."

"And I'm going to have lunch with my
friend Moira," said Mrs Walker. "So we all
have an enjoyable day in store!"

They were all standing inside the new
Tippington Fountains Shopping Centre.

Kirsty was staying with Rachel for the half-term holiday, and they had been having a very exciting time ever since the shopping centre opened. A Design-and-Make Competition had been announced on the opening day, and the girls had been working on their ideas ever since. After the workshop, their creations would be judged, and the winners would model their clothes in a fashion show at the end of the week.

"Let's go this way," said Mrs Walker. "I said that I'd meet Moira outside the wedding dress shop, *Top Hats and Tiaras*."

They walked along slowly, looking at all the exciting new shops on either side. Then Rachel nudged Kirsty.

"Look at that lady over there," she said. "She's wearing one long trouser leg and one short."

"Her son only has one sock on," said Kirsty. "That's stranqe."

"New fashions always seem strange at first," said Mrs Walker with a laugh. "Look, there's Moira over there, and she's got safety pins on her cardigan instead of buttons. Whatever will the fashion designers think of next?"

As Mrs Walker went to give Moira a hug, Kirsty and Rachel exchanged a glance.

"These aren't funny new fashions," said Rachel. "It's Jack Frost and his naughty goblins causing trouble!"

Read Tyra the Dress Designer Fairy to find out what adventures are in store for Kirsty and Rachel!

Meet the
Fashion Fairies

If Kirsty and Rachel don't find the Fashion Fairies' magical objects, Jack Frost will ruin fashion forever!

www.rainbowmagicbooks.co.uk

Meet the fairies, play games
and get sneak peeks at
the latest books!

www.rainbowmagicbooks.co.uk

There's fairy fun for everyone on
our wonderful website.
You'll find great activities, competitions, stories and
fairy profiles, and also a special newsletter.

Get 30% off all Rainbow Magic books at
www.rainbowmagicbooks.co.uk

Enter the code RAINBOW at the checkout.
Offer ends 31 December 2012.

Offer valid in United Kingdom and Republic of Ireland only.

Competition!

Here's a friend who Kirsty and Rachel met in an earlier story. Use the clues below to help you guess her name. When you have enjoyed all seven of the Fashion Fairies books, arrange the first letters of each mystery fairy's name to make a special word, then send us the answer!

CLUES

1. This Princess Fairy has leopard-skin shoes.

2. She wears an orange dress.

3. Her magic item is a tiara.

The fairy's name is _ _ _ _ the _ _ _ _ _ _ _ _ _ _ _ _ _ _ _ Fairy

We will put all of the correct entries into a draw and select one winner to receive a special Fashion Fairies goody bag. Your name will also be featured in a forthcoming Rainbow Magic story!

Enter online now at www.rainbowmagicbooks.co.uk

The Complete Book of Fairies

Packed with secret fairy facts
and extra-special rainbow reveals, this magical guide
includes all you need to know about your favourite
Rainbow Magic friends.

Out Now!